ViVo™

Encore!

Adapted by Cala Spinner • Illustrated by Alex Cho

SIMON SPOTLIGHT

New York   London   Toronto   Sydney   New Delhi

SONY PICTURES
ANIMATION

SIMON SPOTLIGHT
An imprint of Simon & Schuster Children's Publishing Division
1230 Avenue of the Americas, New York, New York 10020
This Simon Spotlight paperback edition July 2021
SIMON SPOTLIGHT and colophon are registered trademarks of Simon & Schuster, Inc.
For information about special discounts for bulk purchases, please contact Simon & Schuster Special Sales at 1-866-506-1949 or
business@simonandschuster.com.
Manufactured in the United States of America 0621 LAK
2 4 6 8 10 9 7 5 3 1
ISBN 978-1-5344-6813-9
ISBN 978-1-5344-6817-7 (ebook)

In Havana, Cuba, there was always music playing and people dancing together in the street. Every day, Vivo, a kinkajou, and his friend Andrés sang and performed in the plaza. They were musical partners, and they were also best friends.

Then, one day, a letter arrived.

The letter was from Marta Sandoval, a famous singer. Andrés and Marta used to perform together when they were younger. Andrés loved Marta, but he had trouble finding the words to tell her.

But then one day Marta was invited to perform at the famous Mambo Cabana in Miami, Florida. Marta followed her dreams and left Cuba.

Andrés never stopped loving Marta. He even wrote her a love song, even though she would never get a chance to hear it.

Now Andrés had a second chance. Marta had invited him to her farewell concert at the Mambo Cabana. She wanted to perform together one last time!

But then, that very night, Andrés died peacefully in his sleep.

Vivo decided there was only one thing to do. He would travel to Miami himself and give Marta the love song that Andrés had written for her.

Gabi, Andrés's great-niece, visited Havana for the vigil. As Gabi was leaving to go home to Key West, Florida, Vivo snuck into a drum case and flew with her.
Vivo was nervous, but he was ready to do anything for his best friend.

Once they arrived in Key West, Gabi was thrilled to discover Vivo. She was even more thrilled to learn about his plans to deliver the song to Marta. But Key West was very far from Miami, and Marta's concert was happening that night.

"You're never going to get there on your own. You need me," she said.

Gabi and Vivo decided to take a shortcut to Miami by going through Everglades National Park.

Gabi was having a great time. In her mind, going on a wild adventure was a hundred times more exciting than selling cookies with her Sand Dollar troop!

Vivo, on the other hand, was terrified. The dark, mysterious swamp was so different from his everyday life in Havana.

"Don't worry, Vivo," Gabi said. "I get scared sometimes, too. My dad used to sing to me when I was scared."

Vivo remembered how Andrés would sing to him when he was scared, too.

Gabi started singing and drumming to cheer Vivo up. Soon Vivo joined in, and the music turned into a full-on jam session! Vivo was so caught up in the beat that he forgot he was still in the scary swamp. He also didn't notice a storm brewing in the distance.

Gabi and Vivo tried to paddle their way through the storm, but they became separated. Vivo found himself stranded in the middle of the Everglades, alone. Even worse, the sheet music to Marta's song was still with Gabi.

While searching the Everglades for Gabi—and Marta's song—Vivo met a spoonbill named Dancarino.

"Excuse me. I got separated from my friend. Could you maybe fly me up and help me find her?" Vivo asked.

Dancarino had other problems on his mind, though. He wanted to introduce himself to his one true love, Valentina, but his shyness was getting in the way. She didn't even know that he existed.

"Dancarino, don't overthink it," Vivo said. "You can do it!"
Vivo helped Dancarino introduce himself to Valentina. It worked—Valentina

Dancarino and Valentina flew away together. Vivo was left all alone in the Everglades again.

"I'll be lucky to get out of the swamp alive, let alone deliver the song to Marta," Vivo said sadly. He drew in a deep breath and yelled, "Gabiiiii!"

Suddenly, a large python named Lutador appeared in front of Vivo. "I can't stand noise," Lutador said. "You must be quiet."
Vivo nodded, terrified.
"Of course you will be quiet," Lutador hissed. "Eventually, all my meals are!"

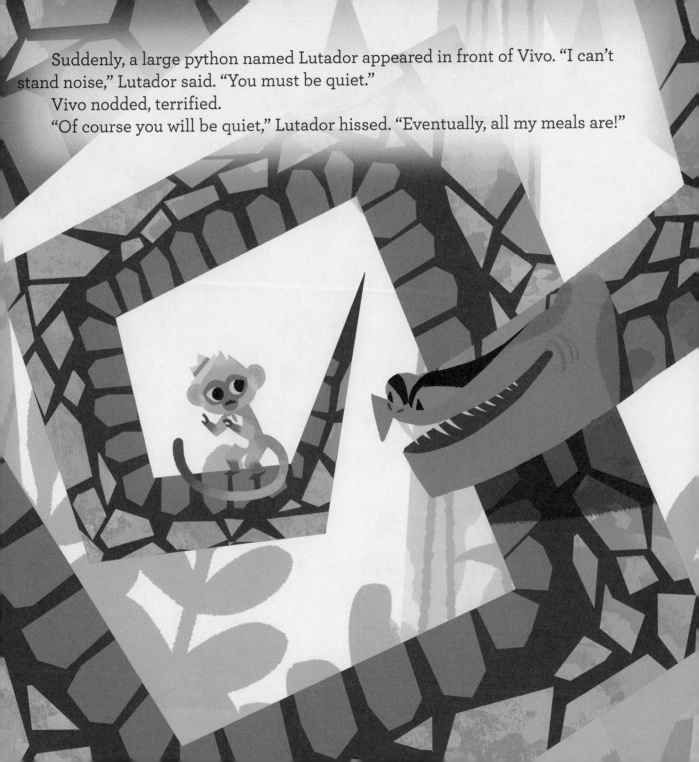

Just when it seemed that everything was lost, Dancarino dove in and swept Vivo away from the python! While Vivo had managed to escape, he was still upset. He was no closer to fulfilling his friend Andrés's wish.

"Don't worry, Vivo," Dancarino said. "We've got your back."

"I promise we'll find your friend!" Valentina said.

Then Vivo heard someone screaming. It was Gabi and the Sand Dollar troop, who had come to find Gabi after she didn't show up for her cookie sale shift. The girls were being chased by Lutador!

Vivo distracted the snake by drumming and making a lot of noise. He had saved the day!

But there was a bigger problem. In the chaos of defeating Lutador, the song had fallen into a puddle. It was soaking wet and totally unreadable.

Vivo was devastated. This had been his one chance to fulfill Andrés's dream, and Vivo had let him down.

Then Gabi realized something. She still remembered the lyrics to Marta's song, and Vivo knew the melody. If they put their minds together, they still had the song!

"The mission for love is back on!" Gabi said.

As they continued on their way to Miami in the Sand Dollar troop's boat, Vivo and Gabi wrote a new copy of the song together.

They made it just in time to Marta's concert. Vivo snuck backstage, where he found Marta crying. She had just learned about Andrés's death.

Vivo handed her the paper with Andrés's love song.
"'Para Marta,'" Marta read out loud. "Andrés wrote this . . . for me?"
Then she turned to Vivo. She still had tears in her eyes, but she smiled. "Thank you, Vivo. Andrés would be so proud of you. I love him too."
Marta decided to sing the love song at the end of her concert.

Vivo had finally fulfilled his best friend's last wish. He thought about Andrés and all the music they had played together in Havana. Then Vivo thought about Gabi, Dancarino, and all the new sights he had seen in Florida.

Vivo still missed Andrés, but he was also happy to be in a new place. It was time for a new life in Florida, full of laughter, music, and new friends. It was time for Vivo to play a new song!